MW01113967

Nolan's Monsters

Written and Illustrated
by
Janice Ramos Tingley

This book is dedicated to

Kory and Kolten with love

Auntie

Copyright © 2018 by Janice Ramos Tingley

All rights reserved. No part of this publication may be reproduced, distributed, or transmitted in any form or by any means, including photocopying, recording, or other electronic or mechanical methods, without the prior written permission of the author, except in the case of brief quotations embodied in critical reviews and certain other noncommercial uses permitted by copyright law.

ISBN: 978-1-64314-612-6 (Paperback)
       978-1-64314-613-3 (Hardback)
       978-1-64314-614-0 (Ebook)

AuthorsPress Publishing
California, USA
www.authorspress.com

At night, about bedtime, my mother would go into my room and read a story until I fell asleep.

Sometimes, when I wake up in the middle of the night,
I would imagine five little monsters jumping on my bed.

My first little monster is a fuzzy, straggly, hairy, round, one-eyed monster.

My second little monster is a fuzzy, straggly, hairy, rectangle, two-eyed monster.

My third little monster is a fuzzy, straggly, hairy, triangley, three-eyed monster.

My fourth little monster is a fuzzy, straggly, hairy, square, four-eyed monster.

My fifth little monster is a fuzzy, straggly, hairy, octagon, five-eyed monster.

There they are. Five little monsters are jumping on my bed!

As I lay here, warm and sleepy, I wonder,
"Do you have monsters jumping on your bed?"

CPSIA information can be obtained
at www.ICGtesting.com
Printed in the USA
BVHW011557070223
658050BV00010B/755